For Alan, Emma, Wilf and Ted, with love x – C.J–I.
For Jemima, with love – S.B.

The yoga breathing exercises and poses in this book are
great for children of all ages – and grown-ups too!
They can help bring a sense of calm, boost energy levels
or mood, or just find a quiet moment in a busy day.
This book has been checked by a qualified yoga
instructor but was not written as a set of instructions.
It was designed for you to enjoy with your child.
Please don't leave children to try poses unsupervised.

First American Edition 2020
Kane Miller, A Division of EDC Publishing

First published in Great Britain 2020 by Red Shed, an imprint of Egmont UK Limited
The Yellow Building, 1 Nicholas Road, London W11 4AN
Text copyright © Egmont UK Ltd 2020
Written by Susie Brooks
Consultancy by Emily Sharratt
Illustrations copyright © Cally Johnson-Isaacs 2020
The moral rights of the author and illustrator have been asserted.

For information contact:
Kane Miller, A Division of EDC Publishing
P.O. Box 470663
Tulsa, OK 74147-0663
www.kanemiller.com

Library of Congress Control Number: 2019936220

Printed and bound in China
1 2 3 4 5 6 7 8 9 10
ISBN: 978-1-61067-990-9

I Breathe

Susie Brooks

Kane Miller
A DIVISION OF EDC PUBLISHING

Cally Johnson-Isaacs

Would you like to discover your own
SECRET SPECIAL POWERS?
All you really need to do is BREATHE!

With yoga, every breath can
take you on an adventure . . .

To the forest like a
STRONG, wise tree . . .

Through the jungle like
a BRAVE lion . . .

Up into the sky like an airplane soaring free! WHEEEEEEE!

Yoga can calm you down, cheer you up, and make you feel READY FOR ANYTHING!

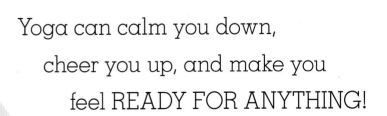

Lulu feels BRAVE, like a fearless lion.
She's not scared to climb up high!

Lulu takes a deep breath, sticks out her tongue,
then lets out a loud, proud ROAR . . .

Imagine you're a roaring LION too!

Feel brave enough
to try something new!

Becky and Ben feel READY, like buzzy bees.
There's lots to do, but they're still CALM.

They shut their eyes and ears,
and gently close their mouths . . .
then they breathe out through their lips with a HUM.

Pretend you are a BEE, fluster free!

Can you stay calm, even when you're busy?

Daisy feels HAPPY, like a playful dog.
She's WIDE AWAKE and having FUN!

She stretches her legs and lifts her hips high.

Dora lifts up one leg . . .

Dan waggles his tail!

Can you pretend to be a waggly DOG?

What makes you feel happy?

Flo and Fin feel LIGHT,
like fluttering butterflies.

They see the bright side,
even on a cloudy day!

They touch their feet together and gently flap their knees . . .

Imagine you are a colorful BUTTERFLY.

Feel light enough to fly away!

Billy feels RELAXED, like a floppy teddy bear.
He's daydreaming about all his favorite things!

With every deep breath,
    his belly lifts and lowers.

        His soft teddy goes up . . .
            then down!

Try resting like a peaceful TEDDY BEAR.

What will you daydream about?

Tess and Tom feel STRONG,
like old, wise trees.

Their worries have blown
away with the breeze.

Tess's roots hold her steady
on the ground.

Tom reaches out his branches as he sways.

Imagine you are a mighty old TREE.

Feel strong and patient, even when you wobble.

Harry feels CHEERFUL, as if
a balloon is floating in his chest.
There's nothing weighing him down!

One long, deep breath in . . . then he gently blows out.

PHWW

Imagine you are a BALLOON, floating in the sky.

WWWWWW.

How high will you fly, and what will you see?

Mo feels CALM, like a sleepy mouse.
He's SAFE in his own quiet world.

He curls his body forward
and stays very still.

Imagine you're the tiniest, quietest MOUSE . . .

Can you stay as still as can be, without making a sound?

Aisha, Amy and Ali feel FREE,
like soaring airplanes. They can
see adventure ahead!

They lift one leg backward and
spread out their wings.

Ali leans his body forward . . . WHEEEE!

Can you pretend to be an AIRPLANE, flying free?

Imagine the places you'll explore!

Alice feels ALERT, like a bouncy bunny.
All her tiredness has HOPPED away!

She takes three short sniffs . . .
then breathes out slowly.

Can you pretend to be a bouncy BUNNY?
Feel full of energy and ready to play!

You can use your yoga BREATHING POWER
whenever you need it.

If you're worried, relax like a TEDDY BEAR!

Fill your belly with soothing air.

When you're busy or flustered, be a BEE.

HUMMMMMM . . . That's better!

Blow away any sadness with a bright BALLOON.

PHWWWWWWW!

Sniffing like a BUNNY can help when you're feeling tired.

Don't be scared or shy – remember your

LION'S ROAR!